Dear Saya

Wish I could
read This Story
To you. t+ oo

Love, Grandma
x x oo

Little Puppy
Saves the Day

Muriel Pépin
Adapted by Patricia Jensen
Illustrations by Marcelle Geneste

Reader's Digest Kids
Pleasantville, N.Y.–Montreal

One cold, snowy day, a farmer brought home a shaggy little puppy. After settling the puppy in his new bed, the farmer went to the market to sell some eggs and vegetables.

Just as the farmer's old car pulled away, all the animals from the barn gathered together and went to the house to meet the new puppy.

The poor little puppy was frightened when he saw all the big barnyard animals crowding into the kitchen.

"What's your name?" mooed the cow loudly.

"How old are you?" demanded the horse.

"What a funny little nose he has!" laughed the pig.

"Let's see if his tail is real," quacked the mean old duck, giving the puppy's tail a tug.

"Ow!" cried the little puppy.

"Leave him alone," said one of the geese. "Can't you see he's just a little puppy?"

"I am not little!" barked the puppy. "I'm a big dog!"

All the animals laughed. "Big dog indeed!" said the turkey.

The puppy leaned against the wall, feeling littler than ever.

Just then Mother Hen came rushing into the house.

"Help me!" she cried, dropping a downy feather on the floor. "My baby chick has run off!"

"We must find her right away—before the fox catches her!" said the pig.

The little puppy sniffed the feather. "Maybe I can find that chick," he thought. "Then they'll see I'm not so little."

While the barnyard animals argued about the best way to find the baby chick, the little puppy slipped out the kitchen door.

The snow was cold under the puppy's soft paws, but he was too excited to notice. Sniffing the icy air, the little puppy began walking toward the barn.

There were so many different smells in the barn! But before long, the little puppy recognized the smell of the baby chick's down. He put his cold nose to the ground and followed the smell to a small hole in the barn wall.

"She must have gotten out through here," the puppy said to himself.

The little puppy wriggled through the hole and looked toward the woods. He took a deep breath and thought, "I'm a big dog now—and I've got to help find that baby chick." He began following the smell of the chick along a path that led into the woods.

The path ended at the edge of a small pond. "I hope the little chick didn't fall in!" thought the puppy. He sniffed all around, but he couldn't smell the chick anywhere.

Suddenly his keen ears heard a little cry from the other side of the pond.

"That must be the chick!" the puppy said to himself. And before he had time to feel afraid, he jumped into the icy water and swam across.

Sure enough, there on the other side was the sad little chick, cold and wet.

"A big duck carried me across on his back," the chick explained tearfully. "But now I don't know how to get home."

"I can take you," said the puppy kindly. "Just hop on my back."

With the chick riding safely out of the water, the little puppy swam across the pond. When he reached the other side, he didn't even stop to shake himself dry. He ran straight home to the farm with the chick.

"Hurray! Hurray!" all the animals
cheered. "The little puppy found the chick!"

Just then, the farmer's car turned into
the driveway. The little puppy dashed into
the house while the rest of the animals
returned to the barn.

As he watched the little chick walk home
with her mother, the puppy felt proud.
From that day on, he didn't feel little
anymore.

Dogs wag their tails when they recognize someone who has treated them kindly. Wild dogs wag their tails to greet the leader of the pack.

There are many different kinds, or breeds, of dogs. A dog whose mother and father are different breeds is called a mixed breed, or mongrel.

Dogs have a very keen sense of smell. Their sensitive noses can detect scents that are too faint for people to notice.